EXPLICIT DADDY'S ADULT

Filthy Hot Stories In Family

VOL.4

by Rebecca Sin

Table of Contents

PLEASING DAD
Daddy and Daughter Story

At age 26, I decided to go after something I had wanted since I hit puberty - I wanted to fuck my dad. I knew how difficult it would be, and how risky, because of how hesitant he would feel, but I had a few things working in my favor. Firstly, I was adopted, so I could argue that only screwing a biological daughter would really be incest. Secondly, I was positive that he hadn't had sex with mom in ten years or more. I had to wonder if he had found anyone else during that time, since I knew mom had caught him once when I was thirteen fucking another woman in his office. Silly daddy, you should have locked the door. And I hoped his deleted search history was as full of daddy/daughter porn as mine was.

I decided that the best way to get him to fuck me was to make him horny for me before he knew who he was talking to, so I made a throwaway email account and sent him an anonymous confession - "Although it can't happen, I wish I could please you. I know it's probably been a while since someone took care of your needs and I wish it could be me. I would happily suck your cock until it was nice and hard, then spread my legs so you could slide into my soaking cunt and fuck me until you came." Maybe I could get him to sext with this mysterious admirer for a while. I could even send him nudes as long as I didn't include my face.

It was unlikely to work out this way, but I had a thought. Maybe if I turned him on enough I could convince him to wait blindfolded in his office for his mystery lover to come and take care of him. Then I could fuck him without him even knowing it was me. I checked the email account obsessively for the rest of the day, and couldn't sleep at night. I tried to satisfy myself with my fingers but it just wasn't enough. I needed a nice, thick cock.

The next day while he was at work, he did respond. "Maybe we can work something out, as long as my wife doesn't find out. Are you one of my clients? I noticed your profile says your birthday is January 1ST, 1990. I assume that's not your real birthday, but are you really that young?"

"I am in my twenties," I admitted, "Why? Not used to fucking younger women? Then maybe my tight young cunt will be a special treat."

"Not that young! And yes, it definitely will. I'll eat you right up. When can we meet?"

"You wouldn't fuck me if you knew who I was," I confessed. We had been emailing back and forth over the course of several hours, and it was now early afternoon. I had an idea. I dressed in a short skirt, a low cut shirt, and the strappy black boots my father said he wasn't sure he wanted his daughter in. Then, I drove to his office and let myself in.

"Oh! Hi, sweetie!" he said. He was working, but I could see he had other tabs open. "What's going on?"

"I was running errands and just thought I'd stop by. How's your day going?"

"Alright. Have a seat! Can I get you a coke or something?"

"Sure," I agreed, and he left the room. I took the opportunity to hurry over and peak at his other tabs. The email conversation was open, along with a porn - "Dad punishes slutty daughter." Perfect. Made sure I was sitting back down and perfectly composed when he came back.

"So what errands were you running?" he asked, sitting down next to me.

"Actually, I wanted to talk to you about something. You know how I broke up with my boyfriend? There's something I didn't tell you and mom, and she wouldn't understand. Can you keep it between the two of us?"

"Of course," he said. I knew that he concealed a lot from her, so it wouldn't be a problem.

"I actually cheated on him. I have a friend who's an older man, in his late forties, and I tried to convince Rob into letting me hook up with this guy, but he wasn't hearing it. I slept with him anyways."

"Okay," dad said, waiting for me to continue.

"I wanted to say that I understand now, about what happened when I was thirteen. What mom found you doing."

"Oh."

"I know how impossible it can be to function when you get so horny for someone. And I'm sure it was even worse for you, since I don't think you and mom were having sex at all."

"Yea, we weren't. And then this pretty young woman practically threw herself at me and -" he shrugged, "I don't think most men could resist an opportunity like that."

"Have you had any other 'opportunities' like that? I'm curious. I won't tell."

"A few times, yea. No one that young since then. I actually, uh, got this email today-" he stopped and looked up at me. Something clicked. "Sweetie? Was that you who sent me that email?"

"Do you want it to have been me?" I teased.

"I don't know." He sat staring at me for a moment. "Did you mean what you said?"

"Yes," I admitted, putting my hand on his leg, "I really did. I've wanted to do that for a very long time." I ran my fingers up and down his thigh. "How long has it been for you, right now?"

"Three years," he admitted. He watched my hand nervously but didn't stop me. I noticed a growing bulge in his dress pants.

"How about you close your eyes," I suggested, "and just focus on how it feels."

"I don't know, sweetie."

I started to undo his pants and after some hesitation he stood up to slide out of them, then watched as I tugged down his boxers. His erection was a bit bigger than average and I couldn't wait to get at it. He sat back down and closed his eyes, leaning back in the chair, and I kneeled in front of him. He gave a shuddering groan as I gave a starting lick from balls to head, then wrapped my lips around the shaft, swirling my tongue in a circle. Then I got to work sliding my mouth up and down his shaft, trying to take a little more each time and then slowly increasing in speed.

"Oh wow" he said, putting his hand gently on the back of my head, "That feels so good, baby."

I gripped a little tighter and kept going, sucking lightly each time I pulled up for added sensation and cupping his balls in one hand. When I needed to catch my breath I kissed and licked along the shaft and then got back to work pumping away.

"Just another talent my little girl has," he murmured, opening his eyes to look at me. I made eye contact with him as I kept at it, and he groaned. "Oh Abby. Oh yes, baby." Eventually he pulled off his shirt, then leaned over to pull mine over my head. "You have such nice tits, Abby," he murmured, rubbing his thumbs across the fabric of my bra before reaching back to unhook it in a practiced motion.

When my bra fell to the ground he pulled me to my feet and put his mouth to one nipple, licking and sucking.

"Mmmm, yes," I encouraged, "That's nice." With one hand he was stroking himself, but with the other he reached up and played with my other nipple. His warm mouth on my tits was almost more than I could handle. My cunt was soaking my underwear with my arousal. "Daddy, oh yes. Oh hell yes. Oh daddy, please...will you fuck me? Please?" He □uickly tugged down my skirt and panties, then gestured to his desk.

"Bend over for me," he instructed.

I bent over the desk and couldn't help but moan when he came up behind me and slipped two fingers into me.

"Hmm, well I definitely don't need any lube. Who knew my daughter was such a filthy little slut. You've wanted to get fucked by your daddy for a long time?" I nodded enthusiastically. "Well here it is." He slid his cock into me and I barely managed to stay up on my elbows as the pleasure washed over me. He started thrusting into me, slow and steady at first, with his hands on my hips. "You're nice and tight, baby."

"Oh daddy, yes!" I moaned, bucking against him as he slowly increased his speed and the power behind his thrusting. Soon his balls were slapping against me and he was fucking me so intensely that I lost all my thoughts in a haze of pleasure and desire which built and built until I reached my first orgasm. "Fuck yes, daddy," I s□uealed.

"Oh, I'm not done yet, baby," he assured me, keeping up the pace. I loved the hot wet sound of impact with every thrust and got lost again. I ended upcoming three times before he grunted and unleashed his hot cum into me. Then he put his arms around me and pulled me into a hug while still inside of me. "Did you like that, baby?"

"Yes, daddy. Thank you. Thank you so much."

HUNGRY FOR ME
Dad and Daughter Dp Story

As I entered the house I knew it would be a great day. My Daddy had made me wear a butt plug to work that day. It had been hard to concentrate in my constant state of arousal, but Daddy had told me to be a good girl and that only he was allowed to take it out. My pussy ached for his big hard 9 inch cock. Well to be honest, all my holes were aching for him.

Daddy and I had been together since a year after my mom died. He was my everything, and pleasing him was something I was more than happy to do.

The house was oddly quiet as I stepped inside. Normally the sound of Daddy tinkering with one of his many projects would great me, yet today it was just silence.

"Daddy I'm home." I yell as I close the door.

No reply came, and I stepped further into the house to investigate. Suddenly I was grabbed from behind and my Daddy's voice whispered in my ear.

"Welcome home Baby Girl."

He pressed himself fully up against my back. I could feel his delicious cock through my skirt and it made my pussy ache for him even more.

"Daddy you scared me." I said as I wiggled my ass back to feel more of the huge cock.

"I'm sorry baby, I wanted to surprise you when you got home. I didn't mean the scare you. how about I make it up to you."

He then started kissing my neck and his big strong hands slowly trailed down my arms and further down to the hem of my skirt. As well as the butt plug, Daddy had also said that I wasn't allowed to wear panties to work, and my pussy juices had made my thighs all wet.

"Mmmmm, yes please Daddy. I've been wanting you all day."

"Tell Daddy what you need Baby."

By now Daddy's hand had pulled up my skirt and was playing with my wet pussy. I moaned and told him exactly what I needed.

"Please Daddy. Feed my cock hungry holes. Fill all of my holes with your cock. Use my holes like the fuck toy I am."

Daddy smiled at me and guided me over to the dining room table.

"It's a good thing Daddy got the replicas ready for you than."

A few months after Daddy and I started fucking, I had told him about the fantasy I had about all my holes being filled with his big hard cock. Daddy had surprised me one day, by having replicas of his cock made, to fulfill my fantasy. It had been the best experience I'd ever had.

Daddy bend me over the table and spread my ass cheeks apart, seeing the butt plug still there, he let his hand reach for the plug and slowly started to ease it out of my tight little ass.

"You're such a good girl. Did it feel good knowing that your ass was stuffed while your coworkers talked to you like normal?"

"Yes Daddy. I felt like such a slut having my ass stuffed at work."

Daddy smiled and set the now free plug on the table.

"I bet you wanted to spread your legs so everyone could see your hungry ass taking that plug. You wanted them to see how hungry you are for cock that you can't even go to work without something filling one of your slutty holes."

"Yes Daddy. I wanted them to notice it so badly. I'm such a slutty fuck toy. I crave my Daddy's big hard cock all the time. Please Daddy, fill my holes with cock. I need it so badly."

Daddy's fingers started to play with my pussy again, making them nice and wet, before pushing them into my little ass. I moaned and pushed back while Daddy reached for one of the replicas. He had gotten one with a suction cup that he placed in front of my face.

"Start sucking it baby girl."

He reached for the second replica, this one he started running over my aching pussy while I started sucking on the delicious 9 inch silicone dildo in front of me.

"Daddy is gonna have so much fun with you baby. First I'm gonna fuck that tight little pussy open, then I'm gonna replace it with the replica while I slam all 9 inches into your sweet little ass over and over again."

I moan at the thought of it and push back on the fingers in my ass a little more.

"Oh, someone likes that idea. Well it won't do to keep my baby girl waiting."

That was all the warning I got before his huge cock slammed into my pussy. Finally I had my Daddy's big cock inside me, as I had been craving all day. He fucked my pussy hard for a while, but one cock hungry hole was still not filled how I wanted it. I pulled my head off the toy in my mouth and looked over my shoulders and moaned.

"Please Daddy, my ass is hungry too. Fill it please. I need all my holes filled. Please Daddy, fuck my tight little ass too. Make your fuck toy take all of those big cocks in her cock hungry holes."

Daddy smiled once again and reached for the special replica he had made. The toy had a cockring added to it so Daddy didn't have to move the toy in and out of my holes by hand. He slowly pulled out of my pussy and pulled on the cockring, before lining himself back up, only this time his cock was ready to fuck my ass. He started out slowly pressing in, making sure the replica was going into my pussy as his cock was going into my little ass. I moaned as I felt the head of his cock and the head of the toy entered my holes.

"Please Daddy. I need more. Use my holes. Slam those cocks into me."

Daddy didn't hesitate to give me what I asked for and slammed both cocks into me over and over again. Happy with having both ass and pussy being used, I moaned and turned back to the toy in front of my mouth.

"Oh baby, your ass is so tight like this. Daddy's cock feels so good surrounded by your ass. You were made to take Daddy's big cock. You were made to be my slutty fuck toy."

Daddy kept slamming the cocks into me and I could feel every inch of them. My body couldn't take it anymore and I started to cum so hard I feared I would black out.

"Oh yeah baby, cum on Daddy's cock. S□ueeze that ass as Daddy gives you what you need."

All I could do was moan, grib the edge of the table and hold on as Daddy used my holes for his pleasure. He fucked me nice and hard for half an hour, making me cum more times then my pleasure filled mind could count. Each time telling me what a good fuck toy I was being for him, and how he couldn't get enough of my tight little holes. I was so happy for making my Daddy feel so good, but unfortunately every good thing must come to an end. I could feel Daddy's movements start to change, as well as feel his big cock start to twitch in my ass. I could also feel myself ready to cum again. I turned my head to the said and moaned loudly.

"Please Daddy. I need to feel you cum in my tight little ass. Give your fuck toy that huge load of cum deep in her ass as she cums all over your big hard Daddy cock again. Use me as your own personal cumbucket. Cum deep in my ass, then plug my ass so your cum doesn't escape. I want your cum Daddy. Please fill me with your cum. Oh god Daddy, I'm cumming all over your cocks again."

As I started to cum, I heard Daddy groan and felt his cum start to explode into my ass. I could feel the huge load filling me up and even wanted it to end.

After he finished cuming, he slowly pulled the cocks out of me and i moaned at the loss. But Daddy had remembered what I said and □uickly pushed the plug from earlier back into my ass, making sure it wouldn't leave my stretched out hole.

I layed on the table trying to calm my body back down after

the amazing fucking I had just received. Daddy had gone off to the bathroom to clean himself up. When he returned, I felt myself being lifted up into his arms and cradled to his chest. A kiss was placed on top of my head.

"I started a bath for us baby. Let's get you cleaned up and then we can go to the bedroom and cuddle while we watch a movie."

I sighed as Daddy placed me in the warm water. My body felt deliciously sore from our activities. Daddy joined me and softly washed my body, while placing kisses on the side of my head here and there. When my body was clean Daddy got out of the tub, picked me up and set me in the counter where he had placed a towel before joining me in the bath. He gently dried me off, before picking me up once again and carried me to our big king size bed. As he joined me in bed I cuddled close to him, laying my head on his chest. Happy and content being in my Daddy's arms.

HOME AND HORNY
Daddy and Daughter College Story

Bruce had been having a tough day at the office, some of the stresses of work were starting to gnaw at him, but fortunately it was just about time to go home. The day was winding down when his phone buzzed... "Babe, I'm heading out for a bit, I have some errands to run" It was Diana (his wife - see part 1 and 2) "I won't be back until late, meeting up with my sister for dinner".

That was disappointing... Diana was usually great at making Bruce feel better after a long week, indeed he had been looking forward to seeing her curvaceous body and getting his hands on her. Four o'clock rolled around and Bruce decided that he'd head home early, he collected his things to head home. 'Just me, some pizza and movies I guess' he thought to himself.

Upon arriving home Bruce noticed a few things were a bit amiss. There were extra shoes by the door, and someone had been in the kitchen making a snack or something. "Hello?" he called. Had his wife set something up? It wouldn't have been unprecedented. He immediately had thoughts that she had sent one of her friends over and went upstairs to see if anyone was up there. Creaking his bedroom door open he looked curiously inside, no one. The bed was made as usual, things put away, except Diana's nightstand drawer was not □uite shut. Strange.

Heading back down to the kitchen to tidy up the small mess Bruce noticed the washing machine in the basement making some noise, beginning the spin cycle he figured. 'That's odd, why would the washer be going?' he thought to himself.

Heading downstairs there was a pile of clothes by the laundry room door, Cassie's (their daughter's) clothes. 'Cassie's home from college?' he wondered to himself and continued through the basement to her room that was still set up for her.

Cassie had gone off to college in the fall, gearing her education to use her years of dance experience to work with kids. Cassie is an amazing girl, bright and bubbly with blonde hair past her shoulders, firm 36DD breasts, a fit flat tummy, nice round ass and amazing dancers' legs. She's 5'5" and maybe 125 pounds.

As Bruce moved through the basement he could hear a buzzing coming from his daughter's room, suddenly a few things clicked in his head, the open nightstand drawer, the buzzing, he was home about an hour earlier than she would be used to him being there. His daughter was using her mother's vibrator right on the other side of the bedroom door.

He was already feeling a little horny, and disappointed his wife wasn't home, but now this, after thinking his wife had sent a surprise. He was surprised alright! And found himself getting hard thinking about what was going on. Soft moans escaped through the door and he could tell she was nearing climax. Of course she had no idea her dad was on the other side of her door. Cassie's moan grew louder, "Mmm God yes! YES!" she shouted.

Bruce couldn't help it, he took out his cock and started stroking it. She was cumming right on the other side of the door. He gently nudged the door and it opened slowly, he could see her on the bed, legs spread, eyes closed, vibrator inside her shaved pussy, one hand squeezing her own nipple. Bruce couldn't help but watch, just last night he had used that vibrator on Diana.

She reached down with her hand and rubbed her clit hard, working the vibrator with the other hand, let out a loud moan and came again, hard, squirting a bit out onto the bed. Bruce backed away from the door after that sight, his cock raging. He needed to take care of this before she knew he had been watching.

Cassie lay there, reveling in her orgasm. So amazing. She

opened her eyes and pulled the vibrator out of her snatch. She then noticed that her door was partly open. A little dazed she wondered why that was. Maybe it was just a draft, no one should be home at the moment. She pulled her tank top back down over her body and slipped on her thong panties to go find out some sort of answer.

Meanwhile Bruce had gone up to his bedroom to get out his laptop, a little porn was the best solution he could hope for at this point. On the way he had grabbed a pair of Cassie's panties out of the laundry pile. In his hurry he hadn't lock the bedroom door. Queuing up a video of a teen girl getting fucked he began to stroke with the panties.

Cassie, vibrator in hand searched the house for the source of her open door, going past the front door she noticed her Daddy's shoes on the mat and his coat on the hook. She gasped, had he been the reason her door was open? Did he just see her cum? She climbed the stairs and could hear faintly the noises of sex coming from her parent's room.

She listened, 'Yes Daddy please" she could hear, and then slurping sounds, Dad was home, and he was watching porn. She slowly pushed the door and to her surprise it glided open. There was her Dad, on the bed, cock out, but hidden by his hand and a flash of bright pink. He was using her panties to stroke his cock. She could feel herself getting wet watching it happen, subconsciously Cassie started rubbing the vibrator against her clit through her panties.

Bruce watched the video of the teen girl slurping on a cock "Mmmm Cassie", he moaned.

She watched her Daddy as he stroked, and hearing her name leaned forward to try to get a better look when she nudged the door a little more and Bruce took notice of her. Their eyes met as they were each masturbating, neither stopped. Cassie felt herself get wetter, Bruce could feel his cock go even harder if that was possible.

Cassie entered the room, still rubbing the vibe on her thonged pussy, coming to the edge of the bed, watching her Daddy stroke his cock. Her eyes widened as she got a look at how big it actually was, she moaned and slipped the vibrator inside herself turning it on. "Did you hear me cum daddy?" she asks.

Bruce nods yes, eyes flicking from his daughter to the teen sucking dick on his screen. "Can I see what you are watching?" Cassie asks as she moves the laptop so she can see. "MMMmmmm Daddy, she looks like me!"

Bruce stops stroking, tossing the panties aside, grabbing Cassie's neck and pulling her down toward his hard cock. She barely needs the help, diving for it she takes it in her mouth sucking and stroking his hard shaft. She attacks it greedily, slurping and spitting on it. "Fuck you are good at that!" Bruce compliments her, "But I need your pussy!" Bruce pulls her up, laying on his back, so that she straddles his face, his tongue licking her slit, squeezing her ass as he eats her.

Cassie, grinding on her Daddy's face begins to moan, and rub her clit with his tongue inside her, she can feel an orgasm building "Yes Daddy, eat me, eat my pussy Daddy". Bruce, happy to oblige, licking fast and furious until he feels his daughter's body spasming on his face.

"MMMMMMMMmmmmmm" she moans as she cums, "Daddy, I need your cock inside me!"

Bruce helps Cassie get off his face and get laid down on the bed. Kneeling between her legs, slowly pressing his cock into her tight shaven pussy. "Mmmm, yes Daddy, yes!" Once he'd pushed all 8.5 inches inside of her Bruce started to rock back and forth. His length sliding in and out of his daughter. Mesmerized he watches it go in and out of her, reaching down to squeeze her tits and pinch her nipples.

"Mmm yes, bite them!" She pleads. Bruce leans down and bites his daughter's nipples, first one and then the other, taking time to lick and suck on each one. As he bites he can feel her squirm and start to cum on his massive cock. "Uuuggghhhhh Dadddddddddyyyyyyy!"

Feeling her tightness Bruce senses he'll cum soon and pulls out, reaching for his nightstand drawer and a condom. As he leans over she bucks and lays him on the bed, straddling him and then guiding his cock up inside her soaking wet pussy. Bruce moans but lets his daughter take charge. She slides his thick member all the way in and then starts to bounce on it, riding it hard.

"Mmmm Daddy your cock is so big!" Cassie says. "Baby, I'm going to cum!" Bruce says "I'm going to cum and I don't have a condom on!" She smiles down at him, twerking on it, "Yes Daddy, fill me up!" Cassie grinds down hard as she feels her Daddy's cock pulse and twitch inside her. Bruce can't hang on any longer, watching his girl ride him, tits bouncing, rubbing her own clit. "FUCK YES" she shivers and start to cum, then squirt. Bruce grunts and starts to shoot his hot cum up inside of her. They both moan and push and squeeze. Cassie in a daze as she comes down from her orgasm, Bruce forcing as much cum as he can into his daughter.

It ends and she rocks on his cock for a moment before sliding it back out of her, she lays on the bed beside him, snuggling.

"Hi Daddy." She says sweetly. "Hi Honey." He replies.

"I think I'm going to like this visit home."

INTIMATE TOGETHER
Daddy and Daughter Oral Story

A very strange turn of events that was, but the outcome was far better than I had expected it to be, and we've been...rather intimate together ever since she came to live with me.

Now, even though my daughter Eden is almost nineteen years old and is able to go off on her own, she's chosen to stay with me to make it easier on herself while she gets through college, and I, of course, have no problem with this at all. And, of course, what we've been doing is only something between Eden and myself. It seemed to be a silent agreement between the two of us not to tell another soul about what we did...and what we've been doing.

Call it taboo to have sex with your own daughter; I know, I know. Wrong. Immoral. Incestuous. Neither of us had seemed to give a flying fuck about that though.

While keeping this little secret of ours inside the house, we still go about our usual business outside, but when the day is finally over...

Sometimes when we're relaxing and watching t.v. together, I'll get a little too handsy and my fingers would find themselves circling her clit.

Sometimes when she showers, I'll sneak in with her and massage and wash her beautiful body.

Sometimes after dinner, I'd sit her up on top of the kitchen counter, pry open her legs, and fuck her right there.

And sometimes, in the middle of the night, when she gets lonely and crawls into bed with me, I'll tell her how much I love her while I bury my cock deep inside her cunt, nice and slow. A little bit too taboo? Maybe just a bit.

I suppose today was simply another one of those days where Eden was feeling stressed out, desperate, and just needed a bit of comfort and release.

After I had come home from running a few errands, I was greeted with screaming and a plethora of colorful curse words coming from Eden's bedroom. "—I don't fucking care! No, you've never done anything to help me, why the hell would I even think about giving you money? —It's not my problem that your record is an utter clusterfuck! —Ah-ah. I came to Dad's house because I didn't want to be anywhere near you, you psychotic bitch!" And then silence. There could only be one person that she would ever speak to like that.

I made my way upstairs and gently knocked on her bedroom door. It was already cracked open a little, and when I opened it the rest of the way, I found my daughter on her bed with her phone thrown across the room. "Your mother, I'm guessing?" I asked her. Her face was beet red and her fists were curled in so tightly that her knuckles turned white and I feared that her fingernails would cut into her palms.

I knew that it had to be her mother; lately, she's been calling Eden and asking for money to either buy drugs, bail her current boy-toy out of jail, or pay her extremely overdue rent. And, of course, when Eden would refuse, her mother would whip right around and say how ungrateful she is, how horrible of a daughter she is, how greedy and selfish and stupid she is.

Her mother, to put it simply, is a colossal bitch.

I stepped inside Eden's bedroom and tried to place a comforting hand on her shoulder, but she shrugged me off. "I'm fine! I don't—ugh, I just don't wanna be bothered right now." She muttered as she flopped down onto her bed with a groan.

I knew better than to try to comfort her now; there was no

getting to her when she had to deal with her monster—I mean, mother. All I did was nod with a small sigh as I glanced at her phone that was now lying on the floor by her closet door. The door itself now had a small, phone-sized dent in it, and the corner of the phone screen was cracked.

I decided it was now best to head downstairs and leave Eden to her thoughts.

Eden didn't come out of her room for hours. It had already gotten late, and she didn't even come out to grab dinner. Occasionally, I would hear a 'thump' or a 'thud' whenever she angrily threw random objects against the walls, but I remained sitting patiently downstairs. Sometimes you just had to let the fire fizzle out before you tried to touch it. This was one of those times.

It was near midnight when Eden finally decided to crawl out of her cave.

I was sitting on the couch, watching t.v. when I noticed her walk out into the living room. I □uickly muted the television and smiled as she solemnly crawled onto my lap and wrapped her arms around me in a desperate hug. "Oh, baby girl. It's okay now. I know you're upset. I know it's infuriating when she tries to put you down like that, but what she tells you goes right out the window. It means nothing. You understand?" I murmured softly to her as I gently rubbed her back.

She buried her face in the crook of my neck, her choppy black hair tickling at my jaw, and I felt her hands grip onto my shirt. All she did was nod her head, but she kept her face hidden to hide the redness in her eyes, and I felt the slight wetness of her tear-stained cheeks and the slight freeze of her metal snake bites touching my skin.

I placed a gentle kiss to the side of her neck. "It's alright now, baby girl. No need to get yourself so worked up." I murmured in her ear.

After a moment, her sniffling stopped, but she kept herself close to me for a little while longer and just relaxed against my body; however, I suddenly felt her shift her weight and sit right on my crotch.

"Oh, baby girl. You're a little too high up there." I muttered as I placed my hand on her thigh to urge her to move back, but she didn't move back down. Instead...she shifted again. And again. That slight movement was starting to get me a little too worked up as she subtly added that friction against my cock.

"Dad. . . " I heard her whisper from where she was hiding.

She must've been doing this on purpose; the way she had positioned herself so her pussy was riding right along the suddenly growing bulge in my pants. And today it seemed as though she had chosen to wear a pair of her more thin-fabric gym shorts.

"Oooh, I see. You've grown just a little bit needy, hm?" I say as I gently ease her out of her hiding spot so I could look at her face. A slight red hue had grown on her cheeks as she nodded her head ever so subtly. I smiled as I gently pushed her blue and black bangs out of her face.

"You're making me just a little bit needy too with the way you're rubbin' on me like that, precious."

I gently lifted her off my lap and carefully lay her on the couch. Then, slowly, I removed her gym shorts, only to realize that she wasn't wearing any panties underneath. Oh, how it always drove me crazy whenever she wasn't wearing anything underneath her shorts.

I tossed her shorts on the floor and gently spread her legs with one hand. It made me throb seeing how she was already wet with need.

"Oh, Eden, baby girl, look at you. You're all wet, precious." I murmured as I leaned down and placed a gentle kiss to her inner thigh. I couldn't help but smirk seeing how she squirmed when the salt-and-pepper stubble on my face tickled her skin.

"D-Dad, mmmh..." She whimpered as she relaxed into the couch.

"Close your eyes, baby girl. Just relax now." I told her as my hand stroked her thigh. God, how soft her skin is compared to my rough hands. It always seemed to make her squirm whenever I touched her this way. I leaned down again, my mouth now level with her pussy as I breathed in her womanly scent. "Oh, Eden, you're so pretty..." I whispered as my lips planted a kiss to her clit and lingered there until they were satisfied with her reaction.

I could hear her purring in pleasure from where I was, and I had just barely gotten started.

It wasn't until I was dragging the tip of my tongue along her slit when she really started to make those pretty little noises that I had grown to love so much.

"A-aahh~ Dad...Daddy...Mmmhh...Aaahha~"

"That's it, baby girl. That's it, precious." I murmured under my breath before I suddenly plunged my tongue deep inside of her cunt, allowing my upper lip to massage against her clit. She gasped and let out a long, drawn-out moan, and her body began to writhe from the pleasure that my tongue was giving her. She had grown so aroused that her juices were now dripping down onto her ass, but I didn't care. Seeing just how nice and slippery I could make her was always a fun game to play.

While my tongue played around inside her pussy, my hands slowly and gently massaged her legs, relaxing the muscles and getting her body into a state of bliss. My hopes were to completely calm her mind from when she had gotten so angry earlier today, and by the looks of it, it was starting to work.

My tongue licked along her slit once more, tasting her, feeling the smoothness of her lips, lapping up the slickness of her arousal. I let out a muffled groan, the sweetness of it tingling my tastebuds. I then kissed the inside of her thigh once more, before I focused my attention to her swollen little bud, circling my tongue around it and listening to all of the sweet little moans and whimpers that she made. It was starting to get to me . . . the way her body writhed, the sounds she made, the slickness of her pussy.

My actions soon became a little more rough, a little needier. I plunged my tongue back inside my daughter's soaking hole and practically buried my face into her aching cunt. I groaned and grunted and licked and sucked until my lips and chin were coated with her arousal, but I didn't stop there. I kept going.

My finger traced along her opening, feeling just how incredibly wet and slimy her pussy was getting. How that mix of cum and saliva was now dripping down onto the couch, but I'd worry about the mess later.

Whenever I'd pull my face away, a string of saliva still connected my lips to her that I'd have the pleasure of licking away. And then I'd get right back to licking. Lapping. Kissing. Sucking.

Eden's hands gripped onto the couch as her toes curled. "Ooohh... Aaah-aaahh... Aahh...hhaaa... Ooh fuck...Dad...Aaah..." Her breath had turned into short, shallow pants. "Ooh... Ooh my pussy is so wet...Aaahh..."

"Mmh...I know, baby girl, I know." I murmured as I gently

slid two fingers inside of her. I scissored them, opening her up just a little bit to draw another moan from her lips. And then I slowly began to move them in and out of her. Goddamn, she was so slick that I wouldn't be surprised if my fingers turned wrinkly after I was finished.

I spit onto her pussy and massaged it in, watching how her cunt and the inside of her thighs glistened and dripped with cum and saliva. I watched as my fingers became completely coated with a thin sheen of cum, and I listened to the sound of how soaked she had really become as I fingered her faster.

Soon I noticed how tense her body was getting and how flushed her skin had become. "Eden, are you going to cum, precious?" I asked as I curled my fingers up against her sweet spot.

She whimpered and panted. "Yes. Yes, yes, yes, oooh~ Aaahhaa~ Mmmmh...mmmmhh...~" I went just a tad bit harder and added a little bit more pressure against her g-spot, and suddenly she was coming completely undone on my hand. She moaned and whimpered. Her body writhed and her breathing came out in hot, heavy, ragged pants. Her hands tightened into fists and her legs tensed, and then the high was over. As soon as her orgasm had come over her, she nearly collapsed into the couch, panting and sweating and soaking wet.

I couldn't help but smile towards her as I crawled up. I gently turned her on her side and slipped behind her.

"Dad?" She murmured through her heavy breaths.

"Oh, I'm not finished, baby girl." I murmured and positioned my face in the crook of her neck, placing a few nips and kisses along her skin.

While I distracted her, I reached down and one- handedly undid my jeans, my throbbing erection springing out and the tip already dripping with precum.

I then reached over and lifted her leg, allowing me to press the tip of my cock up against her soaking hole. Eden whimpered, "Mm-mmh...You're gonna put it inside me?"

"Mhm. You got me a little too riled up when you were rubbin' up on me earlier." I murmured against her ear. While my one hand kept her leg propped up, my other one slipped down and wrapped around her waist, pulling her tightly up against my body.

"I know you're tired now. I won't take long, precious, I

promise." I whispered before I slowly slid my cock inside her. I was big, but her slickness allowed me to slide in easily. I grunted, feeling how my daughter's warm, wet cunt took my cock so well. I began to thrust immediately, holding her in place as she whimpered and moaned.

"Oh, Eden...nnrg...oh you take it so well." I grunted.

Each and every thrust drew a gasp or a whimper from her, and she leaned against my body while I stuffed her full of my throbbing cock.

I kept her like that for a little while longer, held tightly against me while I thrust again, and again, and again, and again. She gasped and panted and moaned and whimpered, feeling how good I felt inside her. She could feel every single ridge and every single throbbing vein, and it didn't take long before my cock was well coated in a thin sheen of cum.

It also didn't take long before I felt that pressure building inside me either.
"Oh, baby girl, hold on a little longer. Nnrrg...I'm gonna cum inside you now." I grunted and began to pick up the pace.

I could very easily hear the wet squelching of her pussy with each thrust I made, and I could very easily feel how her juices dripped down my shaft. The sensations altogether had pulled me over the edge and all of a sudden I found myself cumming deep inside my daughter's pussy.

She leaned back against me and let out a satisfied sigh as she felt the sticky warmth fill her pussy. "Oh god...oh, Daddy, aahh~...it's so much..."

When I pulled out, the mixture of cum and spit leaked and dripped onto her inner thighs.

I breathed heavily and reached around to move her bangs out of her face once again. With a soft kiss to the side of her forehead, I murmured, "I love you, baby girl."

She returned that with a satisfied smile while she turned around and nuzzled against my body, the anger and stress she felt before now completely diminished.

BREEDING DIARY

Daddy and Daughter Breeding Story

I don't recall my exact age first time I saw a pregnant woman but I remember it so vividly. She must have been fifteen months with how big her belly was. "Daddy, that woman is fat," I said tugging on my father's hand as we walked through the bread aisle in the grocery store.

I think the woman heard me because she smirked. "She isn't fat, honey. She's pregnant," my daddy told me after he apologized to the lady.

In the car ride home, my daddy explained what "pregnant" meant. I had so many questions, but the biggest one was, "When can I be pregnant?"

Most of my childhood I loved playing with dolls. I used to ball them up and put them in my shirt so I could imagine what it would be like when I was grown and carrying a baby. Sometimes I'd even put two in there and imagine I was having twins. Daddy always assured me that when I was ready - when I was old enough - I'd get everything I wanted.

I have long blonde hair. I'm thin with soft perky b-cup breasts, and I always catch the boys at school staring at me. I don't exactly dress like a nun. I wear tight tank- tops and very short shorts, most of the time. So, I understood why all those horny boys can't take their eyes off me. While I get a kick out of flirting with them, I know they have nothing to offer. I've been saving myself. I wanted to be pure and perfect for the man who would fill me with his seed. I wanted to make sure that no part of me had ever been touched. I don't know why this mattered so much. It just did. It made my dreams of becoming a mother seem so much more sacred like my body was this perfect unsoiled vessel to be owned and used by the only man who has ever mattered to me.

Yesterday was my eighteenth birthday. And as luck or maybe fate would have it, I happened to be ovulating on that very day. I could feel it. My breasts were a little tender. I had a heightened sense of smell. And, most of all, my pussy was gushing wet the second I woke up.

I wanted to open my eyes to my daddy thrusting his cock inside me, but that wasn't the case. He's too good for that. Even though my horny teen body needed him more than anything, he's so patient and strong. Instead, he took me out to breakfast to our favorite spot. We sat there like any normal day in our regular both, me sitting inside and my daddy sitting next to me reading the paper and sipping his coffee. He had on the cologne I grew up smelling. Every time he flipped the page his scent wafted over towards me making me even wetter. I sat there with my legs crossed using my thighs to rub my clit. Every so often, daddy reached over and patted my head, or touched my face -- once he even massaged my thigh. Each time he touched me I'd let out a little whimper and he'd just smile. "Daddy, I need you," I whispered. "Haven't you've made me wait long enough."

Daddy glanced around the restaurant before whispering back, "This is a very special day, little girl." Then he leaned in and kissed my forehead. "I want to make sure you remember it for the rest of your life."

On the car ride home, his hand rested on my thigh. His strong fingers massaged my soft tender flesh. I slid my fingers between his and moved his hand up my leg.

Inch by inch he grew closer to that place I desperately needed him to touch. Would he tease me and pull away, something he always did when I was about to get my way, like the time when I turned sixteen and he bought me a car? He held the keys above my head and made me jump over and over again to get it. I was so worried this was another one of his games. Finally, his hand pressed against my tight denim shorts. Daddy diligently watched the road as I ground my hips against him. "Can you feel how wet I am through my shorts, daddy?"

"I can, honey," he answered as he made a left turn.

I ground harder and bit into my lip, staring at the man I loved my whole life. He's so handsome with that gray in his stubble and speckled throughout his dark hair. I unbuttoned my shorts thinking there was no way daddy was going to touch me, but I was able to move his hand deep under my lace panties. His thick rough fingers gently massaged my little clit around and around. Oh my god! Applying just a little bit of pressure he had control of my entire body at the tip of his finger. "Britany, you're soaked," he said without looking at me.

"It's because of you, daddy," I answered as I pushed up into his finger, feeling it part my lips and ease inside me.

When he turned into our driveway, I lifted his hand to my mouth. He watched me lick my glistening juices off his skin. Gazing right into my eyes, he asked, "What am I going to do with you, little girl?"

I smiled and answered, "Whatever you want."

He took me by the hand and led me into the house, up the stairs, and into his bedroom. He sat me down on the edge of his bed. "I want you to know something, Britany," he started as he brushed strands of my blonde hair back behind my ears. "I'm so proud of the woman you've become. I really am. I know today is the day you officially become kind of a grown-up, but you'll always be my little girl. I'm sorry if that embarrasses you or makes you feel like I don't see you as you are. It's just how it will always be, I think."

"No, daddy. That's how I want it to be, forever. I never want to be anything other than your little girl." Daddy smiled and then leaned in closer. I sat up straight to meet him. His lips skimmed across mine as he kissed me like he had done so many times before, but this time he lingered and kissed me again, and again, and again. Slowly, kiss after kiss, our mouths opened a little wider, and then a little more. His hands moved up the sides of my body along my arms to my neck until he cradled my face. For the first time in my life, I felt his tongue press against mine, just for an instant before he pulled away.

"I love you so much, honey." He said and then opened wide as he dove back in. Our tongues swirled inside each other's mouths. He hugged me so tight if he hugged any tighter, he might have hurt me. But he knew, he knew exactly what I needed. We broke the connection just long enough for him to pull my tank- top over my head. His hands moved up my back and unhooked my bra. "It feels so good, daddy - to have your hands on my body. Your hands are the only hands I ever want to touch me."

Daddy pulled away and he took me in, looking at my naked chest. "Honey, you're all I want."

He fell into the nook of my neck and kissed. His rough stubble scrapped against my skin as he moved lower over my collarbone. His big strong hand massaged one breast as his wet lips pressed on the nipple of my other. I felt him tug and suck at the same time stretching my skin. My head snapped back and I moaned.

"Did I hurt you?" he asked.

"No, daddy it feels so good. Do it again."

He did, but this time he sucked and tugged with more vigor. With his hand, he pinched and twisted. I had never felt anything like it. It sent energy all the way through my body like all my switches were being turned on at the same time. I reached into my shorts to rub my clit as daddy bit down into one nipple and pulled. Then he bit down into the other. "Yes please, daddy. Do that. Bite harder."

Sucking, kissing, licking, pulling biting, daddy swapped between each breast. I ran my free hand through his hair and grabbed hold. "Your mother used to really love it when I did this to her, too." He said from between my breasts. "She didn't want me to stop until I left hickeys all over her."

"Yes!" I cried out, pushing daddy back into me. "Do that. Suck all over them until they're covered in hickeys."

The harder he sucked on my breasts the faster I rubbed my little clitty. It was the first time I had any kind of sexual experience in my entire life and I didn't want it to stop. I could feel daddy's saliva all over. Goosebumps formed everywhere except where his mouth was. Just when I thought maybe he had had enough he bit harder, making my body squirm, forcing me back into the present. And then I'd drift away again as he gently kissed and sucked. Finally, when I looked down, I saw what he had done. Some hickeys were darker than others, some were bluer and purple, others were tinted yellow. Even at that moment, I knew later I would look at them in the mirror and touch myself. For days that followed I'd be sitting somewhere, maybe in school, and it would dawn on me that my chest had all this evidence that my daddy loved me.

"I love them, daddy. They're so pretty.

Daddy pushed me back onto the bed and then he pulled off my shorts and panties. He picked up my feet to his mouth and kissed them. "Do you understand that when we're done here, you'll belong to me for as long as I live?" He asked very softly before kissing my calves.

I nodded.

"Do you understand that I'm the only man you'll ever have, that you'll be completely devoted to me in every way. In return, I'll always make sure you're taken care of?" He asked before kissing down to my thighs.

"I can't even imagine thinking about another man, daddy. I need to belong to you." He slid his body between my legs and rested my ankles on his shoulders. I continued, "I need your love and strength. I want to devote my life, my mind, and my body to serve you." He gave tender kisses along my thigh. "You could ask anything of me and I'll give it to you, daddy. I mean anything. I don't ever want to say 'no.' I want to unlearn the word. Better yet, I want it to have never existed."

His lips kissed along the edges of my pussy. All he had to do was move a couple centimeters one way or the other and he'd be right where I wanted him to be. I tried moving my hips but his hands gripped hard and held me in place. "I'm yours, daddy. I'm all yours."

Somehow, he got even closer without kissing my pussy. I squirmed and his hands dug into me. "Daddy!" I whined. "I will prove it to you. I want you to use my body over and over again. I want you to keep filling me with your cum until you've marked me- marked me permanently. Claim your property by making me pregnant. Put a baby in your little girl so for the rest of my life I'll always have a part of you with me."

And with that, he buried his tongue deep inside me. I felt it part my lips and enter my tight little pussy. He licked up to my clit and my whole body shimmied up the bed, but he pulled me back into his waiting mouth.

My heels dug into his back as I thrust hard into his face. "Yes, daddy! Oh my god! Your tongue feels amazing. I love it. I've never felt anything like this!"

He licked around and around, slow, then fast. It felt like every part of me was attached to the tip of his tongue. If he applied pressure one way, I felt it in my chest. If he applied pressure the other way, I felt it in the tips of my fingers. "That's it, daddy! Oh my god! Keep fucking me with your tongue."

I ground so hard against his face as this pressure built in my stomach and radiated out over the rest of my body like ripples in a still-glassed lake. But instead of the ripples getting smaller as they moved outwards, inside me they grew until ever one of my cells were in perfect disorder. With both my hands I gripped daddy by his hair and pushed him into me. "Oh my god! Oh my god! Daddy. I think I it's happening! I'm having my very first orgasm!"

For an instant, my body felt suspended and then I came crashing down into the bed. I twisted and turned. I convulsed. I squealed. I needed to get away from daddy's tongue at the same time I needed more of it.

"Daddy, I'm cumming!"

I felt liquid gush from my slit, and out of nowhere, daddy climbed up on top of me. He kissed me with my sweet cum still all over and inside his mouth. Then he pulled his shirt off over his head and unbuckled his belt like his clothes were filled with fire ants. "Are you ready, little girl? Are you ready for your father's cock?"

"I am, daddy. I hope you like my pussy."

I was still cumming a little from daddy licking my pussy when he guided his member into me. He was so thick and hard like he was fucking me with bone. "Oh my god, daddy. I can't believe you're inside me. I can't believe you're fucking your virgin daughter for the first time."

I wrapped my legs tight around his hips as our pelvises ground together. "Am I hurting you, honey?"

"No, daddy. I love having you inside me. I can take it. Fuck your little girl harder. Fuck me as hard as you want." and with that, he pulled back almost all the way to the point his head slipped out. Then he came crashing down, pushing me into the bed.

"Yes, daddy!"

He pulled all the way out again only to slam back into my little hole. "Daddy, I exist to be yours. You always promised I'd get everything I want, and all I want is to belong to you forever."

I dug my nails into daddy's back as he pounded my tight young pussy over and over again. Our bodies slapped together. Sweat formed on our skin. "I want you. I want your seed. Please give it to me. Please breed your daughter."

The more I talked the harder daddy gave it to me. I love that he bit into my neck and squeezed my breasts. I love that he kissed me even as he fucked me. He knew exactly when I wanted him to slow down. He knew exactly when I wanted him to pound me. I felt his cock growing inside me. I felt his head pressed against my insides. "I promise I'll always be your good girl. I don't want to go away to college. I don't want to go out and party. All I want is to serve you. I want you to come home from work and find me standing in the kitchen with dinner almost ready. I want you to kiss my neck and put your hands on my big pregnant belly."

"I want that, too, honey. That will be a perfect life," daddy groaned before kissing me, sliding his tongue deep into my mouth.

I pushed daddy's head into my neck and held him so tight. "Breed me, daddy. Breed your little girl. Come on. I can feel it. Breed your one and only daughter. I know I'm ovulating. My body is ready for you to make me complete. I want to have a daughter for you. Better yet, I want twin daughters. All you have to do is fill your little girl with your seed."

Daddy groaned and gave one final deep thrust. I felt his cock pulse. "I can feel it, daddy." Oh my God! When all that warm liquid filled me up, I knew this was what I was meant for. "That's it, daddy. Don't stop. Push all that cum deep inside your daughter. Spray your seed all you're your little girl's cervix."

Daddy's lips rested on my neck, kissing me, still unloading more cum. Each time his cock pulsed it sent tingles all over my nervous system. "Don't pull out. Keep it inside me. I don't want to lose a drop. I want this to last forever."

We laid there until my daddy went limp. After a while, he rolled off of me and I held my legs up in the air, trying to use gravity to let his seed fall deeper into me. Daddy, barely lucid, groaned, "I really hope my little girl is going to have my baby. I'm going to keep filling you over and over again until it takes."

"Do you promise to keep using my body even when I'm big and pregnant, daddy."

"I promise to never stop using your body - ever."

And with that, I snuggled up next to daddy and he held me so tight with his hand resting on my belly. I already knew that his sperm was swimming towards my ovaries. I knew that I was going to be pregnant from the first time my father fucked me. Daddy began to snore, and I whispered to myself, "This is what I was born for. This is how I want to spend the rest of my life."

SUMMER FOLKS
Daddy, Mom and Son Story

Dina had broken up with me in the late summer right after my junior year had started at Chapel Hill. It was sometime at the end of August - and I was a mess. To make things worse, my best friend Dan had left at the beginning of the semester to study in Barcelona. We skyped a lot but that didn't compensate for anything really. I was in a dark place. Didn't bother going home for Memorial Day. My parents were worried.

My dick had gone limp that fall. Nothing turned me on. I felt like a freak. So I started to go to crossfit and hit the books harder than usual. And I got stoned a lot. A lot. Decided not to shave or cut my hair. It all went by in a haze. Then the doorbell rang. Mom and Dad were worried and had decided on a surprise visit. "If you're not answering our calls, Josh, we really need to talk," Mom said. I was both happy and not happy. Two hippies in their early forties standing in front of me with their open hearts.

They're really cool and very young at heart, but for some reason I had stopped talking with them. Now that I look back, I was genuinely depressed. We had Indian food for dinner and came back and got stoned in my apartment. I broke down and told them what happened. Everything. The fight with Dina was all about sex and sexuality. How she had known from the beginning that I was bisexual. (My parents had considered this but didn't know for a fact.) That she was embarrassed to squirt. (Mom let out a small gasp.) That I had this by fantasy about her, Dan and me. Eating his cum out of her pussy. I was pretty toasted and really on a roll. I couldn't stop myself from talking. "You know. Maybe pissing a little. Fuck, I don't know." (Both of my parents squirmed a little.) "You remember how we used to walk around naked when I was a kid?" I asked rhetorically. "A bush was a bush. I want that kind of life." (They gave me nods of affirmation.) We hugged and kissed as they left. I felt stronger. Woke up the next morning with a boner for the first time in a while. Jacking off felt good. I love the taste of my cum.

I didn't see my parents again until I went home to Asheville for Thanksgiving. Got there Tuesday evening, a good day's head start before my brother and sister, Jim and Courtney, rolled in with their families. After we had seen each other in Chapel Hill, I wanted some time to touch base alone with my parents. The house was slightly lit. I could tell that my parents were probably in the living room which faced our backyard.

"Josh?" My mother called.

"We're in here, but we're warning you now." No real pause

before my dad continued, "We're hanging out in the nude!" He and Mom laughed. Reason enough to laugh, too. They sounded like a couple of nerds taking a dare.

"You're joking right?" I said as I walked into the room. But, no, there they both were, buck naked, on the couch with candles all over the room. The fireplace was glowing. "Holy shit, guys, I wasn't asking you to do this when we talked at school."

"Don't be a wuss, Josh," my dad scolded me gently. "It's warm and comfy. Get out of your clothes and grab some pizza and a beer in the kitchen and come out here to join us. In a little over 24 hours this party will be over."

I dropped my stuff off in my room and stripped down. The house really did feel comfortable. After putting my food on the coffee table next to my favorite chair, my dad got up to hug me. His whole front body pressed against mine as he nestled his bearded face up close to mine. Our dicks were smashed against each other between us. Everything in me stirred. "You look wonderful," he said looking right into my eyes as he held me, and he kissed me on the lips gently. Nothing out of the ordinary except we were both two grown naked and hairy men.

"Hey, c'mon, give your mom a hug, too!" There she was next to us. She snuggled in between me and my dad to embrace and kiss me. I felt her soft breasts against my abdomen and the down of her pubis brushing against my leg. There we all stood for a moment until I broke the group hug to sit in my chair.

And we were still all naked. I chewed on my pizza in silence for a moment. "Well, this is awkward," I stated, trying to break the ice.

My mom explained, "A little, but it'll pass." She paused. "You inspired us during our visit, you know? Your dad and I thought about making a more open space for you. And for us. Again. On the drive back we realized we were missing something and we want it back. I mean, I stopped shaving and look at this!" She pointed to her thick bush, which was actually quite lovely. "We want more sensuality, more play, more intimacy. Healthy stuff."

I realized then that I loved being around my parents no matter what. We smoked a joint together. We laughed and joked. I told them that my sex life was getting better - at least with myself. We talked through my story with Dina again. She hadn't come around.

At one point my mom intervened, "What was all that you were telling us? Gotta admit, Josh, you were pretty frank about, let me see, three-ways, squirting, and golden showers." Looking at my dad, she paused. "It doesn't take too much to surprise us anymore, but you did." I blushed a little but felt ok about what I said. Mom continued, "Were you serious about all of that?"

"Yes and no," I answered. After thinking a little bit, I conceded, "Yes, I was serious. I do think about stuff like that. We all have our shit that turns us on. I didn't want to lie to Dina about it. C'mon, you guys know I'm bisexual. I always assumed you are, too. I think it's a great way to see get along in the world. I want to feel a man and a woman. At the same time. Right in the middle." I laughed.

"Sounds like heaven to me, son," Dad chimed in with a smile. "There is absolutely nothing wrong with that." He was gently pawing at his lap, the fingers of his other hand combing through the coat of hair on his pec.

"Jeez, Chris," my mom playfully scolded her husband now, "boasting's not your strong suit. You act like you were just at it the other day."

"I wish," he replied with a touch of calm melancholy. "And I bet you do, too. No harm in playing with it, Jan." He winked at her and tugged at his pin.

He caught my attention with that. I mean, his sex caught my attention. I became aware of his cock and the fact that he could potentially be filling my ass with it. I studied him now without shame as he and my mom carried on with their happy banter. I noticed that his tool had chubbied up. His nipples were erect under his fingers. He pinched gently them between thumb and index finger from time to time. His breathing was deep. I watched as he lifted his pelvis forward a little. His fingers groped under his balls. I imagined that he was massaging his own taint as he spoke with my mother. They were definitely communicating with each other nonverbally – bigger meanings behind the words. Mirroring my dad, Mom's hand dropped to nestle in her own lap while the fingertips of her other hand grazed the skin stretching from her ear down to her breast. They were turning each other on just talking about fucking. My own dick stiffened. I was feeling sexed and hungry and unapologetic about it.

"I s☐uirt, too, you know. Especially when I'm getting fucked from behind," Mom proclaimed. Their talk was getting nasty. Weird nasty. But, you know, I couldn't give a flying fuck at that point. Naked as I could be, I had laid out my cards. I was grown and my parents were definitely safe. And, to get to the gut, I was horny as hell. My inner voice told me to go with it. Anyway, my dad was happy and hard like Smokey the Bear. He sat back in a pile of cushions on the couch, legs spread wide with knees bent. A drop of dew hung from the tip of his fat bulb. He looked very furry and genuinely content. Man, I love him.

"Well, darlin', probably don't need to look any further for a man to mount. Dad seems ready and rearing to go." I laughed out of both joy and nervousness. The smell of sex was thick in the air.

"So, what do you think, Tiger?" She sounded like a teenage girl on a high school date, which this most definitely was not.

"Happy to oblige," Dad replied cheerily as he worked his way over to where she was sitting.

Some things in life are much more simple than you'd expect. Especially when everyone is ready for them to happen. My dad spread his legs like a man at the supper table and sat back into the couch, big balls heavy and full. Preoccupied with herself and her sex, Mom slowly lowered herself onto his powerful shaft with her back to my dad. He was clearly fascinated with the way her body easily engulfed this part of him. "Hmmh, this is good," he said to us and to himself.

"Hope you don't mind, Honey," my mom said to me. "Cause this train ain't stopping until it hits the station." I grinned at them and shrugged my shoulders. Have at it, I thought. About time.

I loved watching them. He looked strong and patient like a bull. Dark fleece covered his flushed body, ready for the fuck. Their mated crotches drew me in. The thicket of hair and readiness and sensuality. I yearned to bathe them with my tongue, celebrate with them, lick their delight. Right at the spot of their connection. Although they were both into each other, Mom and Dad looked my way. Here I sat, with a hard tool like an oversized drill bit seeping oil. I was in awe. Dumbstruck by their bodies. They both smiled at me lovingly. And then they began to move. Long slow strokes along the full length of his cock. Almost disconnecting and then enveloping fully. I heard the slurping of sex.

"Wanna see? You can come closer." I didn't need her to ask me twice. Shit, I was high - and randy like a dog. I knelt right smack in front of her and Dad on the floor in front of the couch. I could see Dad's strong piston pushing and pulling, all the while held tight by Mom's slick pussy lips. I was transfixed. Mom was rubbing her fingers in circles all around her mound as she rocked. And they both moaned. Her firm titties bounced. Dad's thick fingers held her strongly right and her hip creases. She opened her eyes just a bit and smiled at me. I couldn't help but reach out and touch them. My fingers were drawn to hers and to the puffy lips around her fattened clit. She cried as she watched me do it. And I was greedy. I could feel their heat and gunk and vibration. My hand slid down their bond to cup the seat of Dad's jewels. The pair rested in my palm as she fucked him. Following a hunch, I reached my fingers lower to his bud. Wet with her lube I stuck my middle finger up his hole. Even though they were moving at a slow even pace, Dad came unexpectedly and hard. Right into her as he jacked his hips up off of my digit. His thick wooly nuts heaved as he held on to her sides and pulled her down on his husky prick again and again. They were beautiful.

"Stay in me," Mom demanded. "Don't know about you, Josh, but your dad can keep hard for a while." Phased and dumbfounded I sat back on the floor. She smiled again as she shifted back and forth on his pole, digging her meat into his pelvis. "Ooh, here it comes. Just a taste." She shuddered. I watched as clear juice trickled out of her snatch and down his weighty ballsack where it dripped on the sofa. My mouth watered and I swallowed hard. She spread her sauce all around her thick pubic hair and even licked her fingers. She sighed again and I watched her leak another stream of cum from the middle of her pink ripeness. Dad reached around and slathered his paw in her honey pot. He greased first his beard and then her sensitive nipples with the sweet. My cock fucking ached and dripped precum. I knew I would explode if I touched myself. And on she rode. She looked so fiery in his strong arms and on his sturdy thighs.

As she moaned louder, I knew she was approaching a big peak. "I'm not going to last much longer, baby."

And she couldn't stop whining now. "Aw, fuck, that feels good. Fuck me, baby." My dad plowed her from behind. Mom was bucking. Literally. She threw her head back and lifted her box almost up off of my dad's knob. Their connection looked swollen and hot. Then she pushed down hard again on him with her pelvis. Like a geyser about to explode, she lifted up once more, and, to my surprise, stepped down in front of me and planted her pussy on my mouth. "Jesus Christ," she hollered and started spraying and spraying.

I grabbed onto her ass, held on for my life. I opened my

mouth and let her in. Heaven. I didn't give a shit about the rules. This woman was gushing life and I wanted to drink all of it. Drunk I was. My lips pressed on her spring while I licked out her honey. My head spun and I dropped slowly onto my back - but she stayed with me. Her warmth covered my face until the back of my head rested on the floor. Mom straddled my mouth as I suckled and swallowed. "That's it, baby," she whispered. "You need this, don't you? We want you to be strong." When I tasted my dad's cum running out of my mom's cunt, I thought I was going to lose my shit. I couldn't get enough of her or him. I was feeding on their funk. My cock was a lightning rod crackling with energy and ready to burst. When I felt a warm mouth, my dad's warm mouth, suck in the swollen head of my lonely tool to cover it all the way to the base, I exploded from deep in its root all the way up into the back of his soft throat while howling into my mom's muff.

BALMY BEACH
Daddy and Mommy Story

It was a balmy summer day and I was happy as a clam!! My wife was sitting in the passenger seat and my 19- year old daughter Misti was listening to her iPod in the backseat as we bounded down the road towards Camp Gulf where we had rented a beachfront cabin for the week.

With times being as tight as they have we decided to downplay our annual family vacation and stay within the state, but wanted to have a good time nonetheless so we arrived at the conclusion that a beach cabin would be perfect. At the last minute our son Robby decided he'd rather go camping with a group of friends so it was just gonna be me and the girls.

The three hour drive out there was pretty uneventful, Diane (my wife) fell asleep about an hour into the ride and Misti started to doze a bit herself. Needless to say, they were full of joie de vivre when we got to the cabin and both ran inside to change into swimsuits as I unloaded the 4Runner. I knocked out the chore in short order though and when they came out looking as cute as could be ten minutes later we all decided to go down and enjoy the beach for awhile.

The ladies, giddy with excitement and babbling like schoolgirls, soon took the lead hand in hand as I casually strolled behind. While doing so I took stock of their bathing suits as they had gone shopping for new ones and I hadn't yet seen them. Diane had on a little white bikini style number covered in a gossamer sarong and was sporting a wide-brimmed floppy beach hat. Altogether I thought it was very stylish.

I have always had the hots for her even after 22 years of marriage. She had kept herself in pristine shape and looked at least ten years younger than her actual age of 47. She had shoulder length auburn hair cut in a very contemporary fashion that flowed down to her soft, lightly freckled shoulders which rolled into a lean strong back that faded into creamy smoothness before jutting abruptly back out into the most adorable heart shaped butt you could ever hope to see. I liked her ass even more now than when we first got together because after all these years it had gained little weight and still stood up hard and round (yet delightfully soft to the touch) unlike a lot of women her age who had flabby, saggy asses.

Also, her tits were just great. They too showed little signs of sag again so prevalent on most women in their late 40's. Even having nursed two children who went on breastfeeding for over a year (who could blame them) they still looked amazing and below them was one of the flattest tummies I'd ever seen in my 49 years of life.

Misti's suit however left slightly less to the imagination. She had on a black tankini with a thong bottom. I shook my head as I chuckled to myself not entirely chagrined over the fact that any horned up surfer boy could gawk at her twin moons so easily.

Misti too was a knockout and could very well pass for her mother when she was 19 the only difference being that her hair was a chocolate brown and they wore slightly different hairstyles.

Breaking my inner monologue Diane blurted out, "Oh shoot...I forgot my iced tea. I'll meet you two down there." With that she scampered off while Misti and I continued towards the beach.

We arrived at a spot about 50 feet from the water line, Misti first with me in tow as it had been from the cottage and I think I stopped about ten feet short of her because I noticed a rather unique dragon shaped kite soaring overhead. I noticed that Misti was staring out at the water when my eyes swept back over to her.

I couldn't help looking at her suit bottoms again and the lightly tanned buns, each slightly more than one handful that engulfed it. I had to admit that daughter or no Misti had a cute little ass (oh who am I kidding it was flat out phenomenal!!). While I'm confessing however I feel I should come clean and tell you that this wasn't the first time I'd ogled my daughter's ass. For the last few years I had especially enjoyed her penchant for wearing pajama bottoms everywhere as they allowed her softness and definition to be easily seen and still gave her some "wiggle room" which I definitely delighted in.

As these thoughts were convoluting my mind's eye. I felt a hand wrap around my now engorged manhood which shocked the hell out of me and it was immediately followed by a sultry bedroom voice that said, "What beautiful scenery, eh?" This was followed by my wife's signature cynical chuckle.

At this Misti turned her head toward us and saw her mother holding my obviously erect penis in her hand angled out in her direction. I think she also caught the direction of my gaze (I hadn't averted it). She just snorted and shook her head laughing at our childish and perverse antics.

"Mmmmm...," Diane purred as she gave my cock another squeeze "we're definitely gonna have to do something about this soon." Then she dropped my Johnson (not that it fell very far) and took my hand closing the distance between

Misti and us.

When we were standing alongside of her Diane ⬜uickly pulled us all into a group hug and excitedly said, "Ooooooh I'm just so happy we're all here together. What a great week we're gonna have!!"

I had to agree this week was gonna be a blast, but at that particular moment my mind was more focused on the fact that I had a boner that could slice diamonds that was at the moment slicing into my daughter's stomach. Then as if it could be more awkward for me Diane grabbed my arm and placed my hand directly on Misti's ass. Now, I know Misti hadn't felt her mother place it there and I expected her to freak thinking that her sick old man was grabbing her butt, but she didn't and actually snuggled into my throbbing manhood; it sliding along her belly. At this point I thought to myself, "What the hell...it's not like I haven't been checking her butt out all these years. Enjoy the moment." With that, I let my hand rub and cup her left cheek. I wasn't quite bold enough to let my hand venture to the right and slide along her ass crack but a part of me definitely wanted to.

Then I kissed her on top of the head and then turned my head and kissed my wife on the lips as we all looked at the blue green water and I openly fondled my daughter's ass with my wife's permission and encouragement.

We had stood there embracing and enjoying this tender moment for a good 15 minutes when Misti said, "Do you guys wanna go down and get in the water?"

Diane looked at me and gave a slight wink saying, "No that's okay honey. I think your dad and I are gonna go relax in the cabin."

Little did Diane know that Misti had caught that conspiratorial, naughty wink and had no intention of wasting time checking out the beach now.

***

We parted ways with Misti and it seemed as if we couldn't get back to the cabin fast enough. As soon as we hit the bedroom door we stripped in such a hurried fashion that we'd put those kids on A Clockwork Orange to shame. Before I knew what was happening I was on my back and Diane was impaling herself on what was definitely the most turgid hard on I'd had in a long time.

We started off a little jerky and out of sync due to our uncontainable lust, but years of practice kicked in and soon we had settled into a nice steady rhythm. Diane was riding my dick like she needed cum worse than oxygen, and I was in heaven enjoying her thrashing ministrations and feebly bucking back from underneath. It was after about ten minutes of this that near the point of no return I let my head roll limply to the side of the pillow my eyes at rest in a half open mask of lust.

Though my face was locked in an expression of intense pleasure and my eyes were more closed than open I sighted through our cracked door someone in the hallway watching us. Imagine my surprise when it occurred to me that this voyeur was none other than my sweet, impressionable 19 year old daughter Misti! And more than just on-looking she was living vicariously through our lust! Her hand was shoved into her tankini and she was really going to town on her clit!

I couldn't believe this, first what happened at the beach and now not a half an hour later and Misti's watching her mom and I screw like oversexed teenagers. I started to wonder what might be turning Misti on more just watching us screw or looking at her mom's delicious ass sliding up and down my pole. I decided to test this out by spreading Di's ass cheeks and giving her what would no doubt have been a sphincter shot from her angle.

Sure as I'm telling you this story Misti then removed the tankini bottoms and began wildly grinding them back and forth along her pussy, her face wrought with an impending orgasm. That's when I leaned over to Diane and pulled her down on top of me. I made it look like I was kissing her neck so Misti wouldn't be aware that'd she'd been spotted.

I whispered, "Don't look now, but we have an audience. And get this Misti has her bottoms in her hand friggin herself off! I think she's getting off on your ass!"

"Oh my god!" Diane exclaimed under her breath, "that's sooooo fuckin hot!"

And with that she thrusted her last and came all over my lap in a wailing, cringing orgasm that certainly made her toes curl. As soon as she recovered she whipped her head back to the door. And a shocked and embarrassed (from what we could see of her) Misti bolted down the hall toward her room Then we both heard the door to her room click shut.

"Wow," I thought "she must be as embarrassed as I was

earlier."

Just then as I was about to blow my load Diane hopped off and locked a fist around the base of my shaft. She looked me in my eyes and very sternly said, "Don't come yet!"

I had no idea what she was doing but knew she meant business. I watched her walk to the door and bend over. As she turned back to me she held in her hand none other but Misti's soiled bottoms.

"Look what I found daddy!" She beamed and smiled a naughty smile at me. Then in a shocking move (although very little should've shocked me after the events of today) she brought the garment to her nose and inhaled deeply obviously reveling in the smell of our daughter's cunt.

"Mmmmmmmm...," Diane moaned.

"Here honey...smell how sweet our little girl smells."

She brought the bathing suit to my nose and shocking myself, I took them in my hand and took a deep, man- sized whiff of the amazing scent. What excited me more was the warm wetness that engulfed my nose and crawled up into my nostrils as I inhaled.

I realized that I was smelling my own daughter's cum, and feeling it on my face, and all of a sudden the sensation became too intense and I began to grow dizzy. I took the bottoms away from my face to get some fresh air. As my head cleared so did my vision and once I could see straight, I realized Diane was looking at me.

"Holy shit...," she gaped "I can't believe we're both getting off on this so much! Can you?"

The truth is that I couldn't. We'd certainly never done anything like this before and had never included either of the kids in our sexual fantasies. Even when I would look at Misti's butt it was never for more than a few minutes and even then was more appreciating a beautiful female form than getting off on my own daughter. But this, my friends, was a new animal altogether. I definitely was enjoying sexual thoughts about Misti and it seemed like Diane was too.

"No I can't." I admitted to her "But I'm enjoying myself and I don't wanna stop!!"

With that I again brought the tankini bottoms to my nose and inhaled as if my life depended on it.

"Oh me either...this is hot! I never would've thought Misti would get me off, but when you told me she was watching me..." Diane trailed off.

"Hey...I have an idea," she added. "How about you continue to smell her with your eyes closed while I suck you off? And if you just so happen to slip and call me Misti...well...that would be okay."

Who was I to say no?

I pulled the garment back over my face and leaned back closing my eyes. When first her mouth came in contact with my rod I immediately dispensed with all pretense of a "slip" and said "Oh Misti, suck daddy's cock. Yeah, that's a good girl!"

"mmmmm...," Diane moaned into my cock.

"Oh honey, daddy loves you sooo much"

"Mmmmm...I love you daddy" Misti...er...Diane groaned from around my tool.

"Oh baby," I muttered on as I received the most incredible head Diane had rendered in ages; thoughts of Misti with my cock stuffed down her throat swirling in my head.

I knew I wasn't going to last much longer and when Diane felt my nuts begin to tighten up she stopped sucking and throatily exclaimed, "Tell me when you're gonna blow baby...I want you to cum in her bottoms!"

Well that about did it. The thought of cumming in Misti's bottoms was more than I could handle.

"NOOOOOOOW!!" I exclaimed in a high pitch. Diane yanked the swim suit out of my hands and covered my cockhead with it in one smooth motion. Then just milliseconds before I erupted the biggest gusher of my life I realized I could feel Misti's sticky juices against my cockhead and I knew that I wanted more. I came long and hard spurting over 3 tablespoons worth of jizz right into Misti's swimsuit bottoms.

Diane gave me tender kisses on my stomach while I laid there and recovered, which wasn't happening anytime soon...

But through my haze I did notice movement at our door for a second time that afternoon. Apparently a certain someone had heard our role play and came back to watch. Diane had noticed her leaving as we finished, and balled the bottoms up so as not to spill any of my spunk then gingerly set them down in the hallway before solidly closing and locking the door. Then she laid down next to me with a content smile on her face as we drifted off to sleep wondering just what would happen next...

FAMILY PICNIC
Daddy and Daughter Story

It was the day of our family annual picnic at our house. We spent all day cleaning and cooking getting everything ready for the family to arrive. Finally everyone came, all the aunts, uncles, cousins and grandparents.

I was wearing the new outfit daddy bought for me, you're very strict about my wardrobe and it's always you who buy my clothes not mommy. I love everything you pick out for me. And I love the pretty bras and panties you started to buy for me last year when my breast started to grow. I'm so thankful I have such an amazing daddy who takes such care of me since mommy only cares about herself. You told me to wear the short shorts, something you've never bought me before, the tight tank top with the pretty purple bra and matching panties.

I was so excited to see my cousin Mary, we were so close before her family moved away last year. But the moment I saw her I knew it wasn't going to be the same. Mary grew up, she was four inches taller and her breasts had grown and she lost a ton of weight. She was every guys wet dream and it made me feel ugly and fat. I watched as all the uncles kept talking to Mary and staring at her. I even saw you looking at her when I was looking at you.

Finally everyone started to leave, everyone but mommy's

sisters who always stay to "clean" but they really just drink and bitch about their husbands and kids. I went up to my room to sulk.

You came in, you never knock you told me daddys don't knock on their baby girls room. I was sitting in the edge of my bed when you cupped my face and turned it up. You could see the tears running down my face ruining my mascara.

"Why are you crying baby girl?"

I was looking down, "everyone was looking at Mary and talking to her and giving her all their attention. It was like I wasn't even there."

"Baby girl, what does daddy always say about looking me in the eye."

"That I need to look at you when we're talking, it's a sign of respect." I look up at you.

"Good girl." You stroke my face. "Did you want everyone looking at you?"

"I don't know daddy. But Mary is so different now. She was

telling me about all the guys she dates and all the things they want to do to her and what she lets them and it just made me feel like a baby!"

"What kind of things has she done with these boys?"

"Daddy, I can't tell you that."

As soon as I say it I realize the mistake I made. I must always tell you the truth when you ask me a ⬜uestion. Your hand tightens on my face and you jerk my chin up stretching my neck.

"I asked you what kind of things has she done with boys."

"She says they want to touch her and she lets them. She lets them out their fingers in her private area and their penises in her mouth."

"And you want to do that with boys?"

"Isn't that what you're supposed to do on dates daddy?"

"Baby girl you've never been on a date. You're not allowed to date, right?" My eyes dart to the left and of course you notice, daddy notices everything. "Baby girl, have you been on a date."

"Once" I whisper.

Your grin tightens and I can see your whole body clench.

"When. With who."

"When I slept at Tessa's last month with her cousin."

"And what happened? Did he put his fingers in your private area and his dick in your mouth?"

"No daddy..."

"But there's something you're not telling me."

"I touched his penis daddy, and then all this stuff slipped out and he tried to put his fingers in my special area and it hurt daddy. It hurt so much."

"Baby girl stand up." You step back.

I stand up, trembling. Afraid of what comes next.

"Do you know what happens to little girls who disobey their fathers?"

I want to look at the ground, but I know it will be son much worse if I do. "They get punished daddy."

"Right. Take off your shorts."

I don't ⬚uestion you, I can already see how you're holding back the anger. I unbutton my shorts and push them down now standing in front of you in my tank, bra and panties.

You sit on the edge of my bed.

"It's been so long since I've had to punish you baby girl." You grab my hip and pull me closer. "And I'm sorry for what's going to happen, it's going to hurt, but you broke two of my rules. Three if we count not looking me in the eyes. But you agree you deserve what's going to happen right?" I nod my head knowing I deserve it because I was naughty. "Now tell me what you did to earn this punishment."

"I went on a date. I touched a boy and let him touch me. And I didn't look you in the eye. Daddy?"

"Yes baby girl." Your play with the strap to my panties.

"I also didn't tell you something the first time you asked."

You let my panties snap back into place. "You're right baby girl, and since you pointed it out I won't punish you for it, but don't think that will make this punishment less."

"I knew daddy. I broke the rules, I deserve to be punished."

"Lay across my lap." When I'm how you want me you brush my hair off my neck and message it. "Now baby girl tell me why I'm doing this."

"Because I didn't follow the rules and good baby girls always follow daddy's rules so you need to punish me so I remember for next time."

"How many spankings do you think you deserve?"

"However many daddy wants to give me."

You rub your hand on my ass. "Good girl. I don't think I've had to spank you since you were little, but I remember how."

Your hand comes down hard on my asscheek.

"Ow!"

You spank me again. "Baby girl you know you're not allowed to cry. You deserve this."

"Yes daddy."

You keep spanking me, slapping one cheek then the other, never in the same place twice. My ass gets redder and redder. Soon your forget why you're doing this.

I start to squirm. You stop with your hand midair. "Why are you moving?"

"Daddy, something is wrong." I all but moan.

Now that I've brought you back down you realize that while you've been beating my ass my breathing has grown heavy and you can feel wetness on your legs. It dawns on you that baby girl is starting to enjoy her spankings.

You slam your hand back down on my ass and I let out a loud moan. You start to rub my ass your hand moving further and further south until your fingers find the pussy juice leaking out of my virgin pussy.

"You little slut."

"What daddy?!" I try to get up but you grab my neck and push me back down.

"No wonder Mary's cousin hurt you when he tried to finger you. You like getting spanked."

"No daddy I don't."

You push a finger in me with ease. I moan. "That tells me otherwise baby girl. You're soaking wet and so hot." You pump your finger in and out of my tight little hole. "And so tight baby girl."

"Daddy what are you doing?! You shouldn't do this!" I squirm but you just hold me down.

"I'm your father and I'll do what I want. Anyways, you're a slut, letting some boy put his fingers in you and touching his dick. If baby girl wants to be a slut she can be daddy's slut." You punctuate the words with hard thrusts of your finger. "Tell me this doesn't feel good."

"Daddy, please..."

"Please what baby girl." You pull out of your finger and

circle my swollen clit.

I moan louder. "Please don't stop."

"That's what I thought." You push me to the floor looking down at me as I'm crawling to my knees. You lick my juices off your finger. "If you want to be a slut, you're gonna be daddy's slut."

You grab my hair and force my face into your lap. "You feel that baby girl?" You rub my face against your stiff cock.

"Daddy..."

"That's what you do to me slut." You push harder. "You think I would be looking at Mary when I have you at home. You stupid whore. I've been watching you for years. Waiting for you to fuck up so that I can finally do what I want with you. Make you daddy's little whore. That's what you want right? You want to make daddy happy. Isn't that what you want baby girl?"

"Yes daddy." I nozzle your cock through your shorts.

"Take it out baby girl." I start to unbuckle your belt. "Look at me."

I look up and unsnap your shorts and pull your belt off. "There's my good girl." You rub my hair. "You like being daddy's good girl don't you."

"Yes daddy."

"Good." You stand up letting your shorts fall to the ground, you're cock free from any underpants pops up and hits me on the cheek leaving a wet mark. "Show daddy."

You can see the panic in my eyes. "Just touch me."

I reach up and run my fingertips up and down the shaft.

You hiss through clenched teeth. You grab my hands and show me how to rub your cock.

"Daddy, it's so soft and hard and warm."

"You made it this way baby girl and when you make daddy hard it's your job to make it better."

"Daddy what's that wet stuff?"

"That's daddy's precum it means daddy likes what you're doing."

"Can I taste it?"

"Yes baby girl."

I slowly lick the drop of precum off your dick. "Daddy it tastes so good!"

"I'm happy you like it baby girl cause there's more. If you suck and lick daddy's cock like that popsicle you had earlier you'll get more."

I start to lick around the head of your cock and suck you into my mouth. I moan around your dick at how good you feel. I bob my head up and down.

"Baby girl, you do as daddy says and wants right?"

I nod my head, my mouth too full of dick to answer.

"That's my good girl." You grab my hair and force me down on your cock. I start to choke and struggle, pushing against you to breathe again. "Stop struggling slut, this is what daddy's baby girl does."

You pull my head down four more times. Making my mascara run for a different reason. You finally push me off your dick, but I scramble back trying to get it in my mouth.

"Get up and get undressed."

I □uickly remove the rest of my clothes standing completely naked in front of you. You push me on the bed on my back.

You slap my pussy. "That's for being a slut. You said you've never sucked cock before but you're too good to have never done it before." Slap slap slap.

"No daddy I swear I've never done that before!" Slap. "Please daddy I swear!"

"Okay baby girl, I believe you." You rub my pussy where you slapped it. "You must just be a natural cocksucker."

You reach up and twist my nipples making me moan in pain. Then you lick the pain away and move onto the next one. You reach down to my pussy and collect my juices and smear it on my nipples and go back to licking and biting them; turning my moans of pain into pleasure.

"Since baby did such a good job sucking daddy's cock she deserves a reward." You climb down my body, bringing your face to my pussy. You breathe your hot breath on it making me squirm. You pull my pussy lips apart and attack my clit with your tongue. I scream and arch my back off the bed.

"Shut up slut or I'll have to gag you with my cock again. If your mommy comes in here she'll make us stop. Do you want that?" You ask as you insert a finger into my right pussy.

"No daddy. I'm sorry it just felt so good."

"It's supposed to." You slap my pussy again this time hitting my clit making me jump.

You go back to licking around my clit and finger fucking me. "Pull on those nipples like a good little slut."

I reach down and twist my nipples like daddy did. You go back to licking me, you can feel me growing wetter, you know what's going to happen. You fuck your finger in me faster and faster and suck my clit into your mouth.

"Daddy, I don't think... I don't know... daddy."

You can hear the uncertainty in my voice reassuring you this is my first time cumming. "It's okay baby girl. You're going to cum, it's what supposed to happen."

"Ohhhhhhhhh!!" I bite my lip to keep from screaming. I cum hard, squeezing your finger with my pussy.

You watch my face as I cum and when I'm coming down from my high you sit on my chest and start jerking your cock over my face.

"Now good girls take their daddy's cum. And I want to cum on your face. Open your eyes and look at me baby girl."

I open my eyes and you can see the lust that's still there. You can see you made me into your little slut and I will do anything daddy wants me to.

"Tell me you want me to cum on your face. Tell daddy you want his cum covering your slutty face.

"Please daddy, please cum on my face daddy. Mark me as your slut daddy."

You start to cum and I don't close my eyes, I watch your face as you cum. Once you finish unleashing all over my face you tell me to open my mouth and stick my tongue out. You drag the tip across my tongue getting it all off.

You look down at me and smile as I give your cock little kisses. You reach down and touch my hair. "You're daddy's good girl."

"Thank you daddy."
"Now, I think it's time for baby girl to go to bed." You get up and tuck me into my blankets like you do every night. Only this time I have your cum dripping from my face.

"Good night princess. Daddy loves his baby girl."

"Night daddy I love you too."

You lean down to kiss my head and you whisper "the next time I come into your room I'm fucking your little pussy baby girl. Sweet dreams."

PERFECT MEETING

Daughter and Daddy Story

I'd never met my biological father before. But when I was a teenager, I asked my mom about him and she told me that he lived alone on the outskirts of town. I told her that I was interested in connecting with him. My mom became very worried and said that she knew this day would come.

She said that my dad was a very handsome, very sexy self assured man. She said he had "a way with the ladies"...especially younger ones, which is why he left my mom when she got to be "too old for him".

"I'm not telling you not to go see him, Jordan", my mom said. "Just be careful. Your father can be very...persuasive. He has this irresistible sexuality about him. I can't explain it..."

"Sexuality? Ew! Mom, he's my dad!"

"I know, I know, honey. I'm probably worried for nothing. But I wouldn't be doing my job as a mother if I didn't warn you."

I trusted my mom's judgement, but I needed to meet him and formulate my own opinion of the man. Besides, he was my father. I really didn't understand all the warnings and why she kept telling me to be careful.

So one Friday night I drove out to the outskirts of town to the old rundown house that mom described to me. As I pulled into the dirt driveway, I could see my father sitting on the front porch drinking a beer. When he saw me get out of my car, he stepped off the porch where I could see him clearly in the moonlight.

JEEZUS, I thought. Mom wasn't kidding. My father was a rugged, yet distinguished older man. And yes, he was sexy as hell.

"Hey there little darling," he said as he looked me up and down ⬜uite lewdly. "You're either lost or this is my lucky day."

I guess mom was right about him being a womanizer too. I glanced down at what I was wearing. A skin tight white sundress that showed off all my curves. It was low cut, showing off a lot of cleavage and it clung to the youthful yet bountiful swell of my tits. My nipples were hard in the cool night air and were clearly visible through the thin fabric of the dress. As I felt the cool breeze on my nether region, I was reminded of how dangerously short the dress was. And that I was not wearing panties. I could see the goosebumps forming on my tan upper thighs which glistened in the dim light of the moon.

I looked back up at my father who was still staring me down like a predator looks at its prey. He reached down and adjusted himself in the leg of his shorts. Yet he did nothing to hide the engorged lump that was forming there.

"Well aren't you just the sweetest damn thing these eyes have seen on my front lawn in a long time," he crooned as he leisurely strutted toward me. I don't think he actually ever looked at my face. "Turn around darling. Let me see who I'm talking to here."

I was already facing him. So that just meant that my dad wanted to get a look at my ass. Part of me was put off by his banter. But I was also amused by his brazen confidence.

"C'mon sweetheart. Don't make me beg. You look good enough to eat from the front. But I'm willing to bet that your backyard is something they write songs about."

That comment actually brought a smile to my face and I could feel myself blushing. I put my hands on my hips and slowly turned my back to him.

"Mmm, mmm, mmm!" My dad whistled at me. "When you're right, you're right. But I was wrong. 'Special' ain't the word to describe what you got goin' on back there."

Suddenly I could feel him right behind me. His breath was on the back of my neck as he spoke.

"So which is it?" he asked me. "I don't follow," I finally spoke.

"Are you lost? Or is this my lucky day?"

My whole body was shivering. "I'm...I'm lost", I lied.

"Are you sure?" he teased. "Because I'm sure feelin' damn lucky right about now."

He brushed the hair away from the back of my neck. "Lil' Angel", he read the inscription of my tattoo there. "Is that what you are? An angel?"

I nodded as I could feel his body pressing into me from behind. And then I felt the bow at the back of my neck being pulled. The spaghetti strings that held the top of my dress in place came undone and I reached up to grasp it before it fell. I heard him take a final swig from his beer before letting the bottle drop to the ground.

"Because you are dressed like a little devil," his body forced me forward as I spun to face him. I knew my dress had ridden up as I felt my bare ass press against the cold steel of my car. My dad had me pinned back against it. He leaned toward me and placed his hands on the hood of the car on either side of me. I could feel his bulging cock pressing into my belly. "Why are you here?" he whispered into my ear.

"I...I was..." I could barely form a sentence. This was my own father, pressing his body firmly against mine...trying to seduce his own daughter...succeeding. I knew I needed to stop this. To tell him that he was my dad. But just as my mom had warned me, I was falling prey to my father's advances. I lied again. "I-I told you...I was lost."

"Mmm...You were lost", his hands moved up my thighs and over my hips dragging the hem of my dress with it. "But you aren't lost anymore though. Are you?" I looked up at him, uestioning. He smirked and bent forward. "I found you", he said, his lips grazing my ear.

My head was spinning. I couldn't believe what was happening. I couldn't believe I was allowing it to happen. My dad was kissing my neck. And he had my dress hiked up to my waist when suddenly I remembered I wasn't wearing panties. My hands uickly darted down and grasped his hands pulling my dress back down. But in doing so, I released the top of my dress which he had untied. The material fell away from my chest, baring my now naked breasts to my father. I gasped as he stared at them.

"Well hello", he chuckled. "Don't mind if I do." His head descended as I felt his lips close around one of my nipples. I moaned lewdly as my hands shot up to grab him by the hair. Only I didn't use it to pull him away. I pushed his face into my tit, relishing the feeling of his mouth sucking its nipple, his tongue swirling around it. I pulled his hair and directed his hungry mouth to my other nipple.

My dad's hands were pulling the hem of my dress up again, but this time I did nothing to stop him. I felt the cool night breeze on my pussy. And then my father's hand.

"Someone dressed for the occasion, I see", my father teased as he rubbed his hand up and down on my mound, slipping his middle finger between my slick pussy lips.

"Oh my god", I moaned. "You shouldn't be doing this. This is wrong." My whole body was on fire. And even though I was telling him this, I was opening my legs to give my dad easier access.

"You don't really want me to stop, do you?" His voice was muffled as his mouth was full of my tit. I shuddered as I felt him give my nipple a gentle yet firm bite as he stood up straight and took a step back. He unbuttoned his shorts and let them fall to his ankles. "Tell me you want me to stop."

My eyes travelled down to his groin where his cock stood straight out in front of him. It was absolutely enormous. My father had the most beautiful penis I had even seen. It was thick and long and the bulbous crown. I licked my lips as I watched him reach down and stroke it a few times. My pussy tingled as pre-cum oozed from the tip and dripped onto my bare toes.

He stepped toward me. "Just say the word, darling. And I'll stop." His cock rested on my stomach as he pushed against me. My dad kissed me hard on the lips and I opened my mouth instinctively, allowing his tongue to slip into my mouth.

"Mmmmm," I groaned before breaking the kiss. "We...we shouldn't," I pleaded, while grinding my hips into him. His hard fat dick slid down my tummy, leaving a wet trail as it went. I gasped as it nestled between my thighs, it's head pushing into the groove between my pussy lips.

"Why shouldn't we?" my father asked as he slowly sawed the impossibly long length of his shaft back and forth against my now dripping slit. "Tell me you want me to stop."

I spread my legs further apart, inviting my father between

them. But my dad had other plans. He suddenly spun me around and pushed me down on the hood of the car. I felt the cold metal on my tits as my father yanked the hem of my dress up over my ass.

"Oh my god," I mumbled as I felt my dad swipe the head of his cock up and down between my moist cunt lips, mixing his pre-cum with my juices and spreading them over my aching, willing hole. "This c–can't happen."

"Why not, sweetheart?" he asked as he continued to tease my pussy with his manhood. I could feel him increasing the pressure as he gently pushed forward.

"Unnngh," I grunted as I felt him grasp my ass cheeks and spread them apart. I looked over my shoulder to see my father letting a large portion of spit drizzle from his mouth. I felt it dripping on to my opening, further lubricating my entrance. "Mmmm...because I'm your...oh god...because you're my..."

"Daddy." He finished my statement.

I gasped at hearing the word. Half out of surprise that he knew. Half out of the dirtiness I felt given that I was letting him have his way with me.

"Yes baby, I knew it was you all along," he said as I felt my pussy entrance gradually stretching open to make way for his penis. "You are a spitting image of your mother when she was younger. I knew who you were the moment you stepped out of your car."

"You...you knew?" I exclaimed. "And still you...you wanna..."

"You're damn right I wanna my little girl's sweet tight little pussy," my body shook at the filthy words he used. "You're every bit as sweet and sexy as your mom was...even more so." He inched forward and I felt his massive cockhead pop past my entrance and into my pussy. "But you still haven't told me to stop, have you?"

He held completely still with his hands continuing to hold my ass cheeks apart. His cockhead still just inside the shallow depths of my sex. "I wanna hear you say it," he said.

"W-what?" I asked.

"I want you to tell me what you want, Jordan." I moaned when I heard him use my name for the first time.

"I...I can't," I stuttered. I couldn't bring myself to say the words...to tell my own father to do the unthinkable.

"Maybe this really was a mistake," my dad said as he began to pull the head of his dick out of me.

"Wait!" I exclaimed, pushing my butt back to keep his tip embedded inside me.

"Jordan, do you want me to stop?"

"N-no," I replied after a long silence.

"What do you want your daddy to do to you, Jordan?"

I could feel his hot breath on the back of my neck. I could feel his cock throbbing at my entrance, yet not moving an inch. I could feel my pussy aching for more of his hard thickness.

"Fuck me, daddy!" I finally exclaimed. "I want you to push your hard fat dick inside your little girl and fuck her good and deep until you fill her up with your hot cum!"

"That's my girl," he whispered before grabbing my slender waist and sinking his entire length deep inside me.

"Ohhhhh FUUUUCK!" I screamed. It was so big. It stretched my insides wide and I could feel every inch of him as he slowly pumped his cock in and out of me. "Oh my god, daddy! I've never felt this full before!"

Dad settled into a solid rhythm pulling my hips back into him and thrusting forward hard...slamming his big dick deep into my depths. My father's cock was reaching places inside me that had never been touched before.

"Oh shit! Daddy, you're gonna make me cum!" I announced as my body shook from the top of my head to the tips of my toes. "UNNNNGH!"

He expertly picked up the pace and picked up the intensity as well. As my orgasm wracked through my body, my dad pounded my pussy relentlessly, lifting my lithe body off the ground with each stroke.

"Yes yes yes daddy! Oh fuck, FUCK, FUUUUUCK MEEEE!" I screamed as I felt my daddy's dick erupt deep inside my womb. My orgasm rolled straight into a second one, twice as intense as the first. He held his cock deep in me as his hips jerked uncontrollably...spurt after spurt of his hot seed filling my insides. I was overflowing as his cum seeped out of me from around the root of his shaft, dripping down the insides of my thighs.

When he finally stopped cumming, my dad bent his knees and set my feet back on the ground. His cock relaxed and slipped out of my pussy. A flood of cum and fluids rushed out of me, streaming down my legs. The intensity of it pushed me into another small orgasm.

I collapsed forward onto the hood of the car and my father collapsed on top of me. Both of us breathing hard and basking in the afterglow of the most amazing sex of my young life.

"Oh my god, daddy. That was...amazing."

"You can say that again, sweetheart. You really are something special."

I turned to face him and we embraced. "Mom warned me about you," I told him as I giggled.

"I'm sure she did," he laughed as he kissed me. "I guess she was right to. But I'm glad you didn't let her scare you."

"Me too," I cooed as I pulled away from him and extended my hand to him. "It's nice to finally meet you, daddy."

He smirked and took my hand in his. "The pleasure is all mine, Jordan."

"No it's not," I said as I hugged him tight to me. I could feel his cock hardening against my belly and I reached between us, wrapping my fingers around its thickening girth. "You're getting hard again, daddy."

"Like I said, sweetheart...You are something special," he whispered in my ear as his hands squeezed my ass.

"Do you mind if I call mom and tell her I'm staying the weekend?"

"Shit. She's gonna kill us both."

Our laughter Quickly evolved into moans as daddy pushed his dick into my soaked pussy.

"Oh god yes! Fuck me again daddy! I'll call mom later!"